For my joy-making daughter, Anna, and all her fearless dreams,
and for my mother, Joan Claydon Doyle, our guiding star. – R.D.

For Martha Doyle. – A.L.

First published in Great Britain in 2021 by Andersen Press Ltd.,

20 Vauxhall Bridge Road, London SW1V 2SA.

Text copyright © Ruth Doyle 2021.

Illustration copyright © Ashling Lindsay 2021.

The rights of Ruth Doyle and Ashling Lindsay to be identified

as the author and illustrator of this work have been asserted by them in

accordance with the Copyright, Designs and Patents Act, 1988.

All rights reserved. Printed and bound in China.

1   3   5   7   9   10   8   6   4   2

British Library Cataloguing in Publication Data available.

ISBN 978 1 78344 852 4

Dreams
for our
Daughters

RUTH DOYLE

ASHLING LINDSAY

Andersen Press

Born on this star-scattered night,
kissed by the cosmos —
A child made of moonbeams.

In your small, starfish hands,
the future nestles.
So dream big, little one.

The wind whispers a welcome,
We've been waiting for you
For the joy-making, ground-
breaking magic you'll do.

So never be labelled as
less than you are.
Be brave and believe in
your own guiding star.

Be a daring sea dragon, a wild wolf cub, a proud, free eaglet.

An ocean ranger, mountain-tamer, sky-pirate.

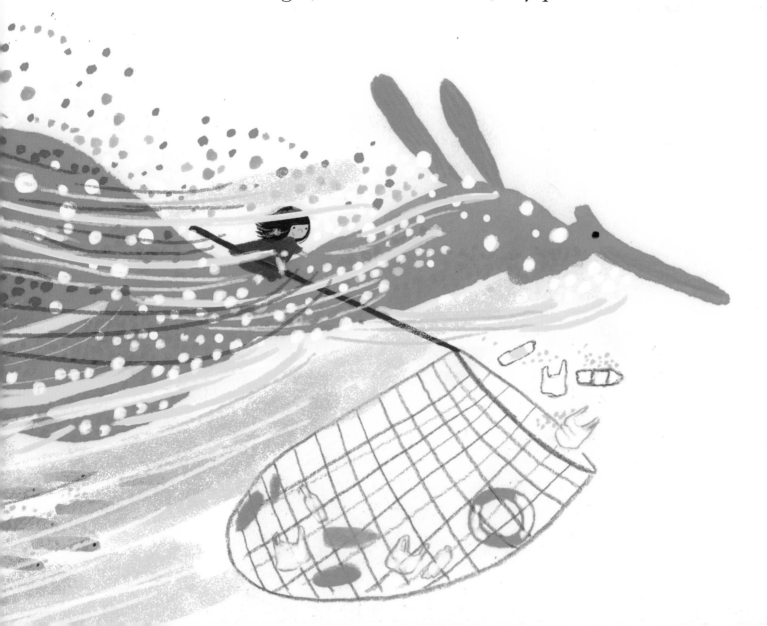

Wear clothes that free you to
dance and to run,
Climb trees, make potions,
run wild and have fun.

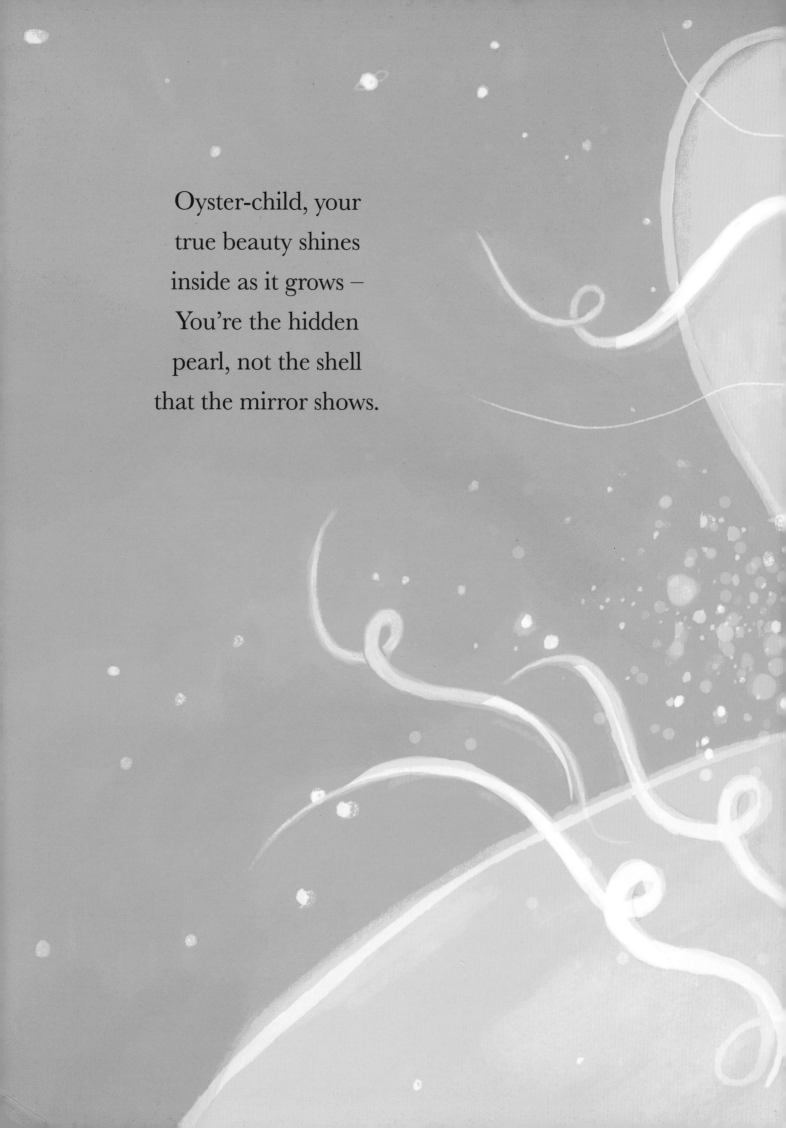

Oyster-child, your
true beauty shines
inside as it grows –
You're the hidden
pearl, not the shell
that the mirror shows.

Be a fearless defender,
a honey bee with armour –
Guarding against the false-charmers
and harmers.

Be a time-traveller, an imagination-navigator.

A dream-maker, sky-painter, story-shaper.

Build bridges,

plant trees,

dig wells,

cast spells,

Be a star-gazer, trail-blazer,
a fire-cracking moon-dancer.

Be a wise warrior, a speaker of truth,

A fierce freedom-leader, a bold self-believer.

Listen in stillness to the unseen worlds,

Hear the cry of felled forests,
the sea's sad song,
The sighs of the homeless
who long to belong.

Become a woodland re-seeder,

an ocean-redeemer

A keeper of kindness and champion of change.

Be a barrier-breaker,
lead your rainbow-nation
In a sky-diving, multicoloured
murmuration.

So get ready for life,
planet earth has been waiting
For the gift that is you and the
hope you're creating.

Stay true to your dreams,
knowing you hold the key
To ignite the bright changes
that you'll long to see.